It's OK To Not Be OK

Accepting When We Are Not OK, And Knowing We Will Be OK.

Written By Kemeasha (Measha Sweets) Brown
Illustrated by Dashaun Murray

This book is dedicated to my amazing God children:
Javiea, Schuyler, Zaryah and Jacob.
+
To my parents Aston and Carlene, thank you for being
the perfect blueprint of what a Mom and Dad should be.
-K.B.

It's Ok To Not Be Ok
KEMEASHA BROWN

Published by Kemeasha Brown
Copyright © 2021 by Kemeasha Brown
First Edition

PAPERBACK ISBN 978-0-578-89195-8

ILLUSTRATION | Dashaun Murray
DESIGN & LAYOUT | Cathryn John | flo-studios.com
PUBLISHING SUPPORT | TSPA The Self Publishing Agency Inc.

About the Illustrator

Dashaun Murray, born and raised in Brooklyn has been drawing all his life. He is an all around artist that specializes in animation, illustration and designing. His main area of focus at the moment is animated content creation. You can follow him on Instagram: @drawnvirus

It's OK
To Not Be OK

I wrote this book because growing up, there were times I found myself not feeling ok, and I often did not say anything because I thought no one would understand. After realizing that I was not alone in how I was feeling, it encouraged me to be more expressive and accepting of my feelings. I want to inspire young readers to be completely Ok if they are having a bad day, knowing that they can find support by talking to their loved ones or friends about what they are feeling.

Always find comfort in knowing that you are not alone and that
It's Ok To Not Be Ok.

-Kemeasha

I woke up today feeling not so ok.

You are enough.

I looked in the mirror and said,
"Kim, why are you so grumpy today?"

"I don't know said myself to myself,
maybe you should go and play."

You can do this.

I went downstairs and saw my mom
and gave her the tightest hug.

I was feeling emotions that I could not
describe, but I knew I would be ok.

You've got this.

I went to the playground and I saw my friends. They all ran to me.

You are loved.

"I'm glad you're here. Let's play kick ball," Joy says with excitement.

"I don't feel like playing kick ball; I woke up feeling grumpy."

"I feel grumpy a lot of times." says Joy "but when I get with my friends and play it, all seems to go away."

You will be ok.

"I don't know you guys I just want to be left alone", mumbles Kim.

"OK, but if you need us, we are here" shouts Shan as she runs back to the field.

"My mom says sometimes it's OK to not be OK and it's OK to feel that way," says Joy comforting Kim.

You are heard.

When everyone left to play, Kim sat by herself and realized that Joy was right.

With the encouragement from her friends and the warm embrace they showed her, she felt good knowing that she was understood.

She often felt like that but did not know how to say it because sometimes when we feel sad, we are afraid to show it.

You are understood.

So Kim got up and said to herself,

"today I do not feel ok, but it will not stop me from having fun because even though I'm having a sad day, I will play with my friends because they too know it's ok, to not be ok."

You are incredible.

And so, Kim and her friends played and played, and when the day was over, they all walked home feeling, ok!

You rock!

When she got home, her mom noticed that she was not looking sad anymore.

"Kim you seem to be in a better mood' I told you that playing with your friends would help," says mom as she waves hello.

"Yes, mom, I am feeling better, but it wasn't the playing that helped me."

"Ok!" Said her mom. "Then what was it?"

You are resilient.

"It's actually who and what was said that helped me." Said Kim.

"Joy said her mom says that everyone will have bad days and sad days too but that it is ok, to not be ok and I felt better."

"Joy's mom is absolutely right."

You are brave.

For the rest of the afternoon, Kim and her mom baked cookies and watched Kim's favorite cartoon.

You are enough.

As Kim sat on her bed, her mom and dad came in and gave her the biggest kiss and hugs.

As they were leaving, Mom turned around and said,

"Sweetheart, whenever you feel like you are having a bad day, know that its ok to feel the way you feel and that tomorrow you will feel better".

One day at a time.

Later that night, before Kim went to bed, she brushed her teeth, looked in the mirror, pointed to herself and whispered,

"Hey you, it's OK, to not be OK".

The End.

You made it.

About the Author

I have always respected Kemeasha's drive and passion for any goal that she sets. She is one of the most focused and ambitious person I have met. She is always willing to share her passion for writing and that is something I admire. - **Sharliemae Henry**

Kemeasha Brown is a passionate, ambitious, and inspirational author who chooses to educate and uplift people through her storytelling. She makes people know that no matter what is going on in their life that things will always get better, to love themselves and love others. I have known Kemeasha for about 20 years, growing up together in church she always wrote plays for the little children and the youth to perform during the holidays, conventions and church retreats.

Kemeasha is a great children's book author who writes incredibly well, she has a great imagination that cater to the minds of both young children and older adults. Her ability to tell stories is to educate, motivate and create self-worth within her readers. Both parents and children can benefit from Kemeasha's work because it opens a doorway for communication. - **Marsha Morris**

I've known this dynamic and extremely talented woman for almost 20 years. Writing has always come naturally to Kemeasha. I remember the many plays she voluntarily wrote for her local church in Brooklyn. It was then that Kimmy, as she's affectionately known, began her playwright journey. Her plays brought joy, laughter and many moments of self-reflection to her audience. I am proud to be able to read her first published book. I know that the readers will be drawn into the story and will eagerly await Kemeasha's next act! I have no doubt that this will be an excellent piece of literature. Congratulations my friend! - **Karon McFarlane**

I have known Kemeasha Brown for over 24 years. She is a selfless individual who is a devoted friend and takes pride in keeping her friends together. I have watched her journey throughout the years in becoming an author and I'm very excited to see her first children's book published and I cannot wait to buy my first copy! - **Sanneika Davis**

It makes me so happy to say that Kemeasha is my friend! She is diligent and very generous. She is an amazing person who takes pride in whatever she sets her mind in and I'm very excited for her path in becoming an author! - **Camella Box**

Kemeasha Brown is an intelligent and ambitious young woman with a passion and love for children. Her passion and desire to help children be confident in who they are is naturally fueled by her love for her nieces and nephews along with time spent caring for children in her daily life. We met when we were 12 years old and it was obvious that she enjoyed story telling and I'm elated to see her passion come to fruition. Congrats my friend! - **Khedeshia Henderson**

I've known Kemeasha all her life and I've watched her grown into this amazing woman. Ever since she was young, writing was always her passion so it's no surprise that this is the path she has chosen. Her writing has brought a lot of joy to others by the plays she has written for her church functions. I'm so looking forward to seeing her growth as an accomplished Author. - **Lorna Heron**

I have known Kemeasha affectionately called Kim all my life. She is my mentor, teacher and a big sister. She is always willing to help anyway she can. Growing up she loved to read and she enjoyed writing. It gave her great pleasure to write and act in plays in our local church groups in Jamaica during childhood years. I knew this was embedded in her. It came as no surprise that she started her writing career to show her affection for kids. I'm excited for her audience to get to know this amazing woman through her books.

I know that her readers will enjoy this book and will eagerly await the next one. Congrats big sis on your major accomplishment! - **Colez Walker**

Kemeasha enjoyed a rather idyllic childhood growing up. No doubt, this has contributed to her genuine love for children and their upbringing, as morally sound human beings. As a young girl, Kemeasha helped to pen several songs when her team prepared for their annual cheerleading competitions. It is no surprise then that she has chosen this path – a Children's Book Author.

With this book, Kemeasha hopes to bring some of her own childhood joys to her tiny readers as they take a beautiful journey between the pages of this book. - **Zelia Gibson Brown**

Ms. Kemeasha Brown, humble, gentle, respectful, hardworking and kind, these are a few of the many adjectives I'd use to describe my past student of many years when she attended St. Mary's College in Jamaica. I was always drawn to her unassuming demeanor and her zeal for knowledge. She embodied a heart of gratitude and showed indelible respect for authority. She was as much my student, as she was my daughter, one I mothered as a teacher and still today refer to her as such. I am not surprised that she has embarked on such an audacious feat and would love to express my sincerest congratulations, with great anticipation for many more great writings from "my child"! - **Keisha Llandell**

Made in the USA
Coppell, TX
20 September 2021

62720859R00021